Sugarfoots Tattle-Tale Series

Sugarfootn' in Ghana -- Why People Have to Work?

Barbara Nyaliemaa Mosima

Illustrated by
Garrett A. Curry

AuthorHouse™
1663 Liberty Drive
Bloomington, IN 47403
www.authorhouse.com
Phone: 833-262-8899

Because of the dynamic nature of the Internet, any web addresses or links contained in this book may have changed
since publication and may no longer be valid. The views expressed in this work are solely those of the author and do not
necessarily reflect the views of the publisher, and the publisher hereby disclaims any responsibility for them.

Any people depicted in stock imagery provided by Getty Images are models,
and such images are being used for illustrative purposes only.
Certain stock imagery © Getty Images.

This book is printed on acid-free paper.

ISBN: 978-1-4389-9375-1 (sc)

Library of Congress Control Number: 2009905699

Print information available on the last page.

Published by AuthorHouse 03/26/2024

authorHOUSE®

"To my son Parker, Nothing is Impossible to the Thinker..."

#6 "Let's go Sugarfoots, let's go", shouted a very excited Babelle to everyone in Sugarfoots village. "Everyone to the circle, we have a very long trip ahead of us!"

All the little Sugarfoots in Sugarfoots' village knew Babelle always had wonderful places to take them to. They quickly hurried to the circle of imagination stones. They were all very excited because they knew they were going to travel to Ghana, West Africa. But, more importantly, they were going to learn a brand new folktale to share with all of their friends!

The Sugarfoots were full of questions. They wanted to know how long it would take to get there and if they needed their coats or their bathing suits! Babelle just smiled at all of the Sugarfoots in the circle, quieted them down, and brought out her traveling map.

1

#6 **W**e are here", she pointed to a big purple "**X**" on the map, "and we have to travel all the way here". Babelle moved her hand across the Atlantic Ocean to get to the continent of Africa and stopped on a big green "**X**". "To travel to West Africa takes as long as having a sleepover party! But lucky for us, in Sugarfoots' village, everything is just a thought away! All we have to do if we want to go to Ghana is close our eyes, reach down and grab a handful of the imagination stones and let's begin;

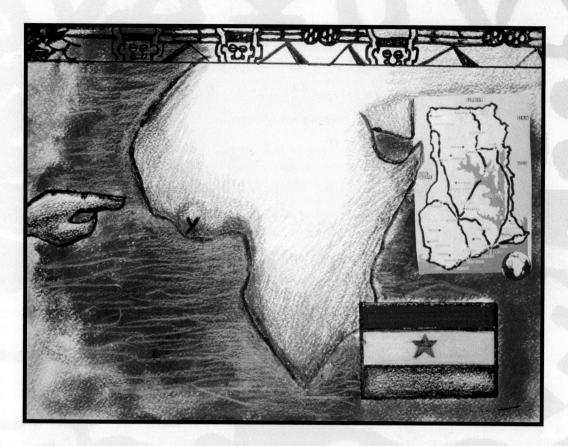

Look to the left,
Look to the right,
Hold your stones
Really, really tight
Nod your head
1, 2, 3
Close both your eyes
And repeat after me

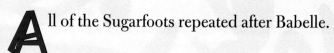

All of the Sugarfoots repeated after Babelle.

Sugar roads and sugar toes
Sugarfoots and all that glows
In my hand the stones will be
And my imagination
Will be with me

Babelle asked all of the Sugarfoots to open their eyes. To their surprise they were standing on a sandy beach in a little coastal village called Keta looking out at the Atlantic Ocean.

"Wow the ocean really does smell salty! It is so hot here. It feels like summer time in July", shouted the Sugarfoots.

#6 I know one problem that needs to be solved," said Babelle, "I am getting very hungry!"

"Well let us not put it off any longer", called out a smiling brown-skinned little girl. "Who are you?" asked the Sugarfoots. "Why I am Abla, a Tuesday born girl. Welcome to Ghana! Welcome to our little coastal village Keta! I have been expecting you and I have a very tasty lunch of fried fish and fresh baked bread prepared for you. But first we must take a short ride on the Tror-Tror to my village Agbozume."

The Sugarfoots were thrilled to meet Abla and they had so many questions. "What is a Tror-Tror? How did you know we were coming? Did you get a message from the talking drum?"

"No", said Abla laughing,"Babelle called me on her cell phone, and a Tror-Tror is a small truck that provides the cheapest and quickest means of transportation to my village. Just make sure you don't step on the chicken's feet if you happened to be sitting next to one being transported on the ride!" chuckled Abla.

Everyone giggled and followed Abla to board the waiting Tror-Tror. The speedy ride on the Tror-Tror showed so many beautiful sights in the country.

There was the greenish blue ocean rippling with white peaks, people walking on the side of the road in bright colored clothing carrying bundles on their heads as high as steps, and so many coconut trees were swaying in the breeze. All of the windows were down on the Tror-Tror and the hot air blowing on them from the ride left them breathless and thirsty.

On the ride to her village, Abla explained that the city of Accra, which is about 120 miles from her village, is the capital of Ghana and it is very busy and buzzing like any normal city.

When they arrived in Agbozume, it was market day.

People were very busy preparing for the business for the day. In the middle of all of the rushing a little girl came up to them with a bucket of water resting comfortably on her head. She began to call out, "I-c-e water, I have I-c-e water to sell". Everyone was amazed at how well she could balance the bucket and did not spill one drop of water!

Abla beckoned her to come and everyone took a cool drink of water from the ladle. She paid the water girl, who quickly moved on her way to the next thirsty customer.

bla had everyone walking down a ginger colored dirt road to her village compound. All of the different homes in the village were surrounded by a four-sided wall, with a double-gated door large enough to drive a car inside! Goats and chickens were casually moving about. One goat became so surprised when one of the Sugarfoots almost awkwardly collided into him, that in a swift moment, the goat leaped over the Sugarfoots' heads to avoid being bumped!

Villagers in Agbozume chuckled to themselves when they saw how such a small goat could startle Babelle and the Sugarfoots! Abla's family were Ewes, one of the many different tribes of Ghana, and her village Agbozume was located in a section of Ghana called Volta Region.

Once they reached Abla's home, they followed her into the yard to sit under the cool shade of a coconut tree. Abla carefully served everyone their lunch on a bed of fresh, wide, green banana leaves that were just as strong as a plate! As they were happily eating their lunch, Babelle turned to Abla and asked her did she have a folktale for them to take back home and share with everyone?

Abla nodded, waited until she had everyone's attention, looked at all of the Sugarfoots and asked them, "Do you know the real reason why people have to work?"

f course everyone thought it was to pay bills or buy toys! Abla smiled and slowly began the tale of the real reason "Why People Have to Work".

A long time ago, in the village of Agbozume (Ah-booze-a-mae), where a great many of Ewe people lived, the sky used to be very close to the ground. Anytime anyone was feeling hungry, all they had to do was reach up and grab a piece of the sky. This was a good tasting sky. It tasted as good as McDonald's french-fries.

The Ewe people, however, became very careless with the sky. They would break off large pieces of the sky and throw the rest to the ground after they had finished eating. The sky did not like seeing him being wasted and thrown all about. The sky told the Ewe people, if they will not be careful he will go away so far, and they would never be able to touch him again. Well they all became very afraid and begged the sky to just give them one more chance. The sky always thought he was a reasonable fellow and he felt everyone deserves at least a second chance and he gave them just that.

Everything was going along just fine. Everyone was eating what they were supposed to eat from the sky and was very careful not to throw him about all over the place. Suddenly, one day without warning, someone no bigger than the size of a chicken took a huge piece of the sky. This piece of the sky was sooooooo big, it could feed everyone on the continent of Africa! Two bites were taken, fingers were licked, mouth was wiped, and the remaining piece of the sky was tossed away!

The sky saw himself lying there on the ground like a worn out popsicle stick. He became mad, I mean really mad, that he went so far, up, up, up so high, that no one in the village could reach out to him again. The next day when everyone woke up from sleep, and were hungry and were looking for something to eat, and they could not find the sky, what do you think they had to do?

#6 "They had to work", cried out the Sugarfoots! Abla shouted with excitement and said, "Now you know the real reason why people have to work!"

"Abla, that was some story", Babelle said, "I do not believe anyone back home really knows the real reason why they are working. I think they think it is all because of money!"

Everyone began to laugh! Babelle noticed the sun was beginning to set, and it was time for her and the Sugarfoots to return back to their own village.

he warm evening twilight embraced them like old friends as they stood up, stretched and prepared to go.

The late afternoon merchant women had slowly gathered in the village market place and had already begun setting up their night tables to sell last-minute suppers for those who were now passing home. At each table, kerosene lamps were flickering in the night's breeze displaying all of their wares of fried fish, bread, and rice.

In the early evening light, the glowing restlessness of the flames in the night outlined a trail and gave just enough brightness for Babelle and her Sugarfoots to follow. They all said their good-byes, hugged and thanked Abla for a wonderful visit to her country, Ghana.

Babelle led the Sugarfoots down the trail. When they turned the corner, they found themselves walking on their very own trail towards the Sugarfoots' village.

The End for now ...

A TATTLE-TALE OR TWO TO TELL

- Accra is the capital city of Ghana

- It takes approximately 12 hours from Washington, D.C. to travel to Ghana

- The climate is hot and humid, except for a few months of the year that is the rainy season.

- The official language spoken is English.

- There are approximately 144 different tribal languages in Ghana alone.

Ewe Children Names of the Week

THE GIRLS	DAYS OF THE WEEK	THE BOYS	DAYS OF THE WEEK
Adzo (Ad-zoe)	Monday	Kojo (Koe-joe)	Monday
Abla (Ah-blah)	Tuesday	Koblah (Koe-bla)	Tuesday
Aku (Ah-coo)	Wednesday	Kwaku (Qua-coo)	Wednesday
Yawu (Yeow-woo)	Thursday	Yawo (Yeow -wo)	Thursday
Afi (Ah-fee)	Friday	Kofi (Koe-fee)	Friday
Ame (Ah-mee)	Saturday	Kwame (Qua-mee)	Saturday
Kwasiwa (Qua-see-waa)	Sunday	Kwasi (Qua-zee)	Sunday

About the Author

Barbara Nyaliemaa Mosima is a graduate of Howard University's Drama Department, with a Bachelor of Fine Arts Degree and has also taught at the Duke Ellington School for the Performance Arts. She is an accomplished actress, comedienne, storyteller and entrepreneur, and has performed throughout the Washington metropolitan area and the East Coast.

Ms. Mosima founded Sugarfoots in 1992, a company that designs cultural soft-sewn rag dolls, created in the three complexion shades of Cocoa, Ginger and Cinnamon. She has been featured in The Washington Post, numerous local news broadcasts, Latina Magazine, Family Digest and thrice in Essence Magazine. Along with Sugarfoots dolls, the Sugarfoots family includes children's books, storytelling workshops and a performing arts summer camp.

Ms. Mosima was a principal performer in the No Neck Monster Theatre Company's production of Sanctuary D.C., nominated in 1988 for the Helen Hayes Award. In the Washington, D.C. comedy-drama production of An Oral History of Tarawaga County, Ms. Mosima's performance was reviewed as "A Goddess of a Black Woman, with warmth and style". She continues to be well noted for her bright comic performances. She has worked with celebrity artists such as Ruby Dee, the late Ossie Davis, Patti Labelle, and Bill Cosby. She is a dedicated and committed performer and delights audiences wherever her path may lead her.

Through Sugarfoots, Ms. Mosima has performed storytelling workshops for the Girl Scouts of America, Jack and Jill, Boys and Girls Clubs, Schools, Museums, the Outreach Children's Theatre Company's touring production of The Golden Journey and Interact, a children's touring production throughout the Washington metropolitan area. With this rich blend of theatrical talents, Ms. Mosima brings to the art of storytelling a unique fusion of improvisation, movement and comic overture. She resides in Washington D.C. with her husband Gabriel and her son Parker.

Printed in the United States
by Baker & Taylor Publisher Services